The Miracle Boy

A Short Story for All Ages

THE RED PLUME PRESS

Petrolia, Ontario, Canada

The Miracle Boy

By Gerry Van Hoorn

The Miracle Boy

A Short Story by Gerry Van Hoorn

Copyright 2019 Gerry Van Hoorn

First Print Edition December 2019

ISBN: 978-1-989346-07-5

Cover Photo by Clement Chai

https://unsplash.com/@clementchai

Dedication

I dedicate my book to my Heavenly Father.

In His Name, everything is possible.

Preface

You may have read or seen on a media outlet, how some little children are treated or how they experience terrible ordeals in their young lives and the way they are growing up. Children who are not so fortunate to have a family, with a mom and dad or perhaps not even to have any parents. Some children have no family at all. Many children who are victims of war carry mental scars.

One of these children is Bart, a five-year-old boy who is an orphan. His parents were killed in a war-torn country. A lady found him walking along a dusty road and brought him to the authorities of the town.

After a few years in an orphanage, where he met his mildly intellectually disabled friend Nihya, he was put on a farm as a foster child where the owners would take care of him, and this would be the beginning of his future. He never forgot the promise he had made to his friend Nihya. As a young child, Bart was treated fairly on the farm, but he had to work like a farmhand to learn to earn his living. Bart, however, loved the farm animals and he did get used to his new environment.

This story will take you through his life.

The Miracle Boy

Chapter 1

The air was full of dust and the little boy looked confused and disoriented. He walked along a dusty road where there was not much traffic. A little child lost and not knowing what had happened to him. He was not crying but he was looking so sad. A car, going in the same direction, stopped ahead of the boy. A woman stepped out of the car, and she approached the little boy and asked him where he was going. The boy did not answer the woman. She took him gently by the hand and walked him to her car.

She put him at ease and tried again to find out more about him with some questions like,

"Where do you come from?" and "Where are your mammy and daddy?" and "Where are you going?"

The boy answered in a child-like way that he did not know what had happen with his mammy and daddy because they were sleeping and did not move anymore although their eyes were open. He said that he was so scared and he did not know where he was going.

The woman could almost cry and she asked what his name is. He answered that his name is Bart. The woman said that her name is Doris.

She said to him that she would take him to a place where he would be safe. Bart went with her into the car and they drove one hour away to the next village. He sat quietly and was looking at the dashboard of the car. You could see that he had no idea what was happening to him or he was not thinking at all. He was totally confused and did not care what was going on.

They arrived at the hospital of the village. Doris told Bart that they were going to see a doctor. He just nodded with his head that it was good.

Inside the hospital, they had to wait and Bart was looking around at all the people who were waiting and at the nurses. Doris took his little hand and she had difficulty to keep her tears. Such a lovely and beautiful child and she was wondering what would be his future. Would it be easy if she just could take him home with her? She realized that was just a dream.

After talking to the doctor, and quick medical exam, they were told to go to the children's centre where they would further take care of Bart. Doris took a little business card out of her purse and gave it to Bart. She told him to keep it safe in his pocket and whenever he needed help, he could call the telephone number at the card. She said "Please don't lose it" Bart looked at the card and put it in his pocket. He gave her a big hug.

Doris took Bart to the Children's care centre and made sure that they would take care of Bart. She gave her name and address to the authorities and asked them to contact her and to let her know what would happen to the little boy. She told them that she would like to adopt Bart when it was possible. Bart was taken away and Doris left with a sad feeling and suspicion that she would never be contacted and never would see the little boy again. Bart, the little boy, was so frustrated and he felt the same way as Doris. He felt attached to her and he liked her so much.

Bart was sent to an orphanage where he would stay for a few years until they could find a foster family. The home he would stay at was an old building, with a few large bedrooms, a cafeteria, kitchen and a kind of recreation room. One was a bedroom for little children and the other was a bedroom for older boys. Bart slept beside a boy who was somewhat, but not noticeably, intellectually disabled. He right away became friends with this boy and they would stick together for the time Bart was in the home.

Chapter 2

Life in the orphanage was not easy for the little boys; they were quiet often harassed and bullied by the older boys. The supervision in the home was not that great because there were not enough volunteers to take this job. Bart learned to avoid problems and to defend his little friend, whose name was Nihya. Bart was taking care of Nihya from the time they woke up and until they went to bed. He helped Nihya to wash himself, to brush his teeth and to brush his hair. They would eat together in the cafeteria. Sometimes, one of the older boys would try to take their food away or slap them on their heads but Bart kept his cool and after some time, they left them alone.

When the weather was good and not cold, the boys would play outside with some other children or they would go for a walk with the supervisor. Inside, they played games and Bart learned to read. At night, he would read stories to his little friend. Even when he could not read all the words, he just fantasized so that it sounded like it was real. One of the supervisors brought some books for the boys and he was happy to see what Bart was doing for his little friend. They both grew up together like brothers

. There would be a time that Bart and Nihya would be separated, which would be a terrible situation for Nihya, because he was so used to being with Bart. The supervisor told Bart to let Nihya know that one day they would be going their own ways and that they would have to take care of themselves. Bart did not want to think about it. He could not imagine what would happen with Nihya. Sometimes he had overheard the stories of the older boys about where they have been before and the way they have been treated in different places for orphans. Bart could not sleep thinking about this.

Photo courtesy of Public Domain

At the Orphanage

Nihya and Bart when they were in the orphanage.

More children were coming into the orphanage and that meant more space was needed, which was not available. So, some of the older boys would be going to foster homes, when those homes became available. Something happened in the home which gave everybody a big scare. Some of the older boys were told that they were going to a foster home, but they did not want to go. One of them tried to set the home on fire. Luckily for everybody, one of the supervisors noticed the fire in time and he prevented a disaster.

Another day, some older boys were fighting and there was no supervision at that time. Bart and his little friend were frightened that the fight would escalate and that they would be in danger. From that day on, life in the orphanage was getting worse and Bart and his friend had to be more careful, especially during the night.

New children coming into the home were not easily getting used to the home and sometimes cried through the night. Bart thought about them, and what might have happened with their families. He realized that he had no mother and father himself and didn't know of any other family, either. He still remembered the little house they used to live in and the beautiful tree in the garden with chickens walking around. All this was destroyed by war and he was lucky to be alive. He did not understand why all this had to happen. He felt somewhat lucky to take care of his little friend.

The food in the home was getting scarce and it was not great quality, but they were getting used to it. Bart had a difficult time to make sure that they were not pushed out of the line up and to make sure that he and Nihya both had enough food. It was getting more and more difficult to live in the orphanage. Bart did not give up on his little friend Nihya. He tried to tell him that one day they would be separated but Nihya did not want to hear about it. Strangely he never showed his real feelings. It was just something he did not understand or comprehend.

Chapter 3

Days and months were flying by and pretty soon, there would be a big change in Bart's life and in the life of his friend, Nihya. Very important people from the town who were overseeing the orphanage were coming to reorganize and to make living in the home a little better, but it came too late for Bart and his friend.

Bart was told he was going to a foster home on a farm, an hour away from where they were living. Nihya was going to a mental facility which was also an orphanage. It was a very emotional situation when the boys had to say good bye to each other. Nihya was crying so much and he kept a hold of his friend so tight that Bart could hardly breathe. It was so sad for both of them.

Bart told Nihya that he would never forget him and when he was older and had his own place to live, he would come to get him. At that time, it was just children's talk and it would probably be forgotten when they were older. But for Bart however, it would be a promise that came back as a memory in the later years.

Chapter 4

Bart was growing up in a work environment but not without a little love and passion. When he was 8 years old, he was sent to a farm and placed in a farmer's family as a foster child. There were two more boys and one girl in the family and they were all foster children. He learned that nothing came easy and nothing was free and that he had to earn his living, just as the other children on the farm. The foster parents were poor but strict and honest people.

Everyone had their own chores to do. The oldest children had already finished school and had to work during the day. Bart had to work in the early mornings and again after he came back from school. He had to look after the animals, which he did with pleasure. Bart liked the animals at the farm, especially the big horses. He was not scared of them. He had to clean the stalls and while he worked, he talked and sang children songs to them and after a while they became used to him. Often, they would stick their noses to his face just to let him know that they loved him.

Sometimes, Bart snuck some pieces of apple to the barn to treat them. He brushed the horses while standing on a wooden crate and they loved his singing. He also loved the chickens and other animals; the little goats and he learned to milk the cows. Even though it was hard work, he still had the time to play with the dog, Max, a Saint Bernard, who was crazy about Bart. So, he forgot all the less happy things he experienced before but he did not forget his friend, Nihya.

He learned to pray from his foster mother Mushwa. She had a Christian background, and every night he would pray for Nihya. He often thought about what he could do when he was grown up. He learned that he himself had to wait and that all things will come through in time when you trust in God.

He went to school during the day and for the rest of the day, he had to do his chores at the farm. On the weekends, he had to work but at night, he could study. He was a good student and he learned to read and to write very easily. He made lots of friends and sometimes he would think of Nihya and where he would be and how he was doing. He had told the lady teacher about him and that he had big plans. That when he was older and had a job and was making enough money to live on his own, that he would go to find his friend Nihya and look after him.

The teacher was amazed with so much trust the little boy had in the future. She had so much respect for him; he was so different than the other children. She loved her job as teacher and she tried to help all the children in her class. Every child had his or her experience in this war-torn country. There was so little hope for the future of the people of her country. She herself was so lucky to have a job; the pay was just enough to live on. She enjoyed teaching the children and gave them hope and love. Her mom and dad were living in the big city and she phoned them every month to keep up with how they were doing.

Chapter 5

The days went by so quickly. In only two more years, Bart would finish school.

One night when he was in his bed, he was thinking about the lady who had brought him to the children's centre years ago. He remembered that she had given him a little card that he had kept in his socks all these years. Only when he had to take a bath did he put it in his clothes. There was a telephone number on the card but he could never make a phone call because he had no money. He never thought of asking his foster mother Mushwa if she had a telephone. When he took the card out of his pocket, he could see how much the printing had faded but luckily, it was still readable. He took a piece of paper out of his school book and wrote the telephone number on it so he could save it in case he lost the card. He kept the little paper in his school book.

On his assumed birthday, (Bart did not know exactly when his birthday was), when he was in school, the lady teacher asked him what she could do for him and Bart had asked her if she could make a telephone call for him. She did not know what to say and she had to think about what he was asking but when she looked in his eyes and saw that he was serious, she asked him why.

He told her about the lady named Doris and that he would like to let her know where he was. She wrote the telephone number that was on the card on a piece of paper and promised that she would make the phone call that night. Bart was happy and he hoped that the teacher would not forget her promise to him.

Later that night, the teacher did not forget her promise to Bart.

Chapter 6

Doris worked as an aid worker for Unicef and when her visa expired, she had to go back to her home in Canada.

That night she could not sleep, she was thinking about the little boy Bart and wondering what had happened to him. When she left the children's centre four years ago, she had given her name address and other information to inquire about the possibility to adopt little Bart. She also gave Bart her name and card with her name, address and phone number and told him that whenever he was in trouble or he needed help to try to get in touch with her. Doris never did receive any information about the whereabouts or the location where Bart was placed. She lived in a town that was 4 hours by car away from the town where she had brought the boy. The road to this town was not without risk but the times were slowly getting better.

The next day she made a phone call to the children's centre for some information but they told her that the boy was in a foster care and could not give her anymore details. Doris was so disappointed that she could not do more to locate

Bart. She decided to go, the next week, to the town where Bart had been in the orphanage.

What happened next was a miracle from heaven.

That night when she was at home from work, Doris had a phone call from Bart's teacher and when she told Doris about Bart, she could not believe her ears! Right away, she asked the lady all about Bart and where he was living. She thanked the teacher and told her to say "Hi" to Bart.

The next day at work, she asked for all the information and forms to adopt a child. As a Unicef worker, she had lots of assistance from higher officials. She had a good chance to adopt a child as long as the local government would agree to the adoption. Maybe it would cost her a lot of money but she was not thinking about that yet.

The time was very short because her term of working for Unicef would be over soon. Everything was set in motion and many phone calls had to be made. All things and forms had to be translated in the language of the country of Bart's birth. It all took longer than they were expecting but there was great cooperation from the different authorities. Doris was so full of expectations of good news that it would be a great disappointment if something went wrong. She did not realize that this was only the beginning of a long journey.

Chapter 7

When Bart went to school that morning, he had a pleasant surprise. His teacher told him that she made the phone call. He was so excited and wanted to know all about it. The teacher had to calm him down a little bit before she told him that Mrs. Doris said "Hi" to him and that she was coming to visit him soon. Bart had tears in his eyes and he thanked the teacher for her help. He almost wanted to give her a big hug but he did not know if he was allowed to do so. His teacher was delighted to see the happiness in Bart's eyes. It gave her a warm feeling and she was happy that she had made the phone call she had promised to make on his behalf.

After school and doing his chores, Bart told the mother what had happened and she was happy for him. Before, when they were alone, Bart had told her about his life and about his friend Nihya. He also told her that when he was old enough and could find a job that he would take care of his friend. The mother enjoyed Bart's optimism and she would pray that his wish would come true.

The mother of the foster children liked Bart and she would miss this little boy so much when he ever went away. She was not able to bear children herself. Her husband needed the foster children to do the work because he could not find man to help him. She loved the children and treated them as her own. She and her husband were of the Christian faith but it was not practised by her husband. She always tried to tell the foster children to trust in the Lord and he will always keep you safe and help you through life. All the children loved their foster mom and dad. They were happy to live at the farm.

Chapter 8

Bart was still in school when Doris visited the farm. She talked with the mother and told her that she was hoping to adopt Bart. It would take a few months before she would know if Bart was allowed to go with her. There were so many unknown government regulations to pass. To adopt a child from any country was very difficult and sometimes very expensive. Mushwa was sad that maybe Bart was leaving her but also happy that if all went well, he would have a better future with Doris, who looked to be a good woman who had never forgotten Bart. She was happy that it would still take some time before she would know what will happen but for now, she could give all her love to Bart every day.

When Doris left Mushwa, she told her that she would come back for a visit if she was welcome to do so. Both women agreed. Mushwa could not speak English but Doris was able to speak in her language so they could get along very well. Later, Mushwa was thinking, what if she adopted Bart? But she put the thought away because she knew that her husband would not agree with this. She could not stop thinking of Bart. The good thing of all of this was that Bart would have a better chance in life and be to fulfill his promise to take care of his friend Nihya.

She found peace in her heart and she would continue to pray for Bart.

Chapter 9

When Doris went to the government office and was directed to the person who had looked over her papers for adoption, she was welcomed by a friendly lady. She put Doris at ease and started to read all the information about Bart and the information about Doris. She said that the adoption would be accepted under one condition; that whenever a legitimate family member came looking for Bart, she would have to return with Bart for a consultation.

The work Doris had done for the country with Unicef had helped her a lot. Doris was so happy and said that she would do so with pleasure and she signed the papers. She thanked the lady with the promise to stay in contact with her and that she would make a donation to the orphanage where Bart had been.

It would be another couple of months before she could take Bart with her to Canada. So much more had to be done and papers to be sent in, for the permanent resident card for Bart because he was not a Canadian citizen. Doris got another extension to her stay and work with Unicef. Her work took her mind off Bart.

The situation in the country was stabilized and no war was going on. Still, traveling in the country was not always safe. It was time to go one more time to the town to pick up Bart. Hopefully nothing bad would happen. All the forms and papers were in her name, Doris Morgan, and Bart's last name was now the same as Doris'.

Chapter 10

Time to Say Goodbye

It was an emotional goodbye, not only for the foster parents but also for the other children when Bart was leaving with Doris. He gave, with tears in his eyes, his foster mother a big hug and promised to write to her as much as he could. He made one more trip to the horse barn to wipe their noses and gave Max a hug and shook his paw. He had so much to tell to Doris about his life and that he was excited to go to Canada. But first, they had to go to the town and to Doris' apartment to prepare for their trip. Lots of things had to be done but first of all, new clothes had to be bought for Bart which was not easy because there were not many clothing stores in the little town, but they found what they needed. The apartment had to be cleaned and made ready for the next person who was going to take over the Unicef work from Doris.

Some personal things had to be shipped to Canada and other minor things taken by air plane. Bart and Doris were getting more acquainted with each other and Bart asked Doris if he may call her Mama. Doris felt tears in her eyes and she was so happy and told him to do so. They were reunited in a special way.

Chapter 11

It was time to go to Canada, back to the home where Doris lived in St. Catharines, Ontario. For Bart, it was an adventure going on an airplane for the first time and to another country. The flight would be very long, 8 hours. It was a short drive to the airport and when they arrived, Bart could not believe what he was seeing. All the big planes and the busy traffic he had not seen before.

The only thing to do was to park the car and bring their luggage to the terminal. Their seats were already booked and they waited to board the airplane. So far, everything went smoothly and since there was no delay, they were in the air in 20 minutes.

The flight went according to the time schedule. They had comfortable seats and the plane was not full. In the air, Bart slept most of the time. When Doris looked at Bart, she still could not believe how much he had changed. She was thinking of the time when she had brought him to the children centre. He still had to learn to speak English but that would come when he went to school.

She was thinking about her own life and how she was a single woman who had no experience raising a child. When she was a teenager, she had a boyfriend but he moved away with his parents to Europe and after that, she had not heard from him anymore. Through her work and church, she had some friends but never got into a relationship so she never got married. Now she had become a mother! Life sometimes turns out in a miraculous way like the slogan, "From the concert of life, you never get a program."

She needed the guidance of the Lord, her saviour.

Chapter 12

Arriving in Canada

Bart could not believe his eyes when they were driving to the home of his new mama, Doris. He looked at the beautiful highways, the tall buildings and all the commercials. It was already late in the afternoon when they arrived on the street where Doris' house was located. It was on a quiet street well decorated with trees in a suburb of St. Catharines. Friends of Doris had taken care of the house while she was away and made sure that all was ready for Bart to stay at his new home.

When they were settled and their entire luggage unpacked, they were quite tired. Doris had ordered some takeout food for dinner and then it was time for Bart to go to bed. For the first time, they prayed together. They were thanking the Lord for all their blessings and their safe travel.

Bart could not sleep well in his new home and he was thinking of his friend Nihya. Would he see him again one day?

Chapter 13

The beginning of a New Life

Bart went to an international school for foreign children of all nationalities to learn the English language and also to keep their native languages. At 10 years old, he had an advantage because learning at his age was much easier. The school was not that far from their home. The first year, Doris would bring Bart to school and pick him up at the end of the day. Doris went back to working at her job at the office where she worked before going abroad.

So, life in Canada took its course for both of them but for Bart, it was not that easy. He could not get used to the school he attended. There were too many children who were affluent and from different upbringing.

After a few months, when the new school year started, Doris decided to enroll Bart in a Canadian grade school, which was a lot better for him. He felt more comfortable with the other children and he was learning the English language much faster than at the other school. Bart needed much help from Doris and his teachers to catch up with all the different subjects in his class. This was his second last year in grade school and he would like to go to college someday. Every night he worked on his studies and had no time for other things. He had to learn the English language which was not that easy, but being in Canada and having to speak English all day, he learned fast. In school, his classmates were eager to know his native language and about the country he came from. (Later, he would become a translator for other people because he did not forget his native language.) Every month, he wrote a letter with some pictures to Mushwa to tell her about how he was doing. Sometimes, he thought fondly of when he was at the farm and of Max and the horses. Soon, he would go back to see them, but first he had to finish his grade school and after that, hopefully college. He knew that he must work hard and do his best.

The years flew by and with a very good report from grade school, Bart was accepted to the college in their city.

Chapter 14

Bart was enrolled in college to study Accounting, Business and Management. He took a part-time job working in a hardware store to make extra money for his future plans. He had asked Doris one day, when he had vacation from school, to go back to his home country to find Nihya.

He told her that he wanted Nihya to come to Canada so that he could look after him when he finished college and had found a job. Doris was not so happy with the idea and she told him not to put his hope up too high because it would be very difficult thing to do, but she promised Bart to help him in any way. She made sure that he knew what it takes to sponsor a person to come to Canada. He would have to take care of his friend for 5 years, which could be very expensive if something went wrong. But Bart was not discouraged; he had promised his friend.

Bart was ready to live on his own but Doris wanted him to stay with her for a little longer. All plans were set in motion for Bart to get his friend Nihya to Canada. Bart had to sponsor him and take care of him for five years before Nihya would be able to get the necessary social benefits, which was a great responsibility for Bart. Doris had much respect for Bart; he had accomplished so much already in his young life. She was so proud of her son but also, a bit worried.

During the vacation of his last year of college, Bart and Doris decided to go for a visit to the country and town where Nihya was living. They booked the trip with friends from Unicef who were going to the same place. Bart was looking forward to this trip and he was hoping for a good result from his visit.

Chapter 15

After Doris and Bart arrived at the airport, they had to drive to the town where Nihya was supposed to live. They had phoned a friend of Doris to pick them up from the airport and drive them to the town. In the time they had been away, lots had changed in Bart's home country and it was not all for the better. Still, they had hope that they would find the place where Nihya was last sent, the orphanage for intellectually disabled children. The civil war in the country was not over yet but they were in the relatively quiet area.

The ride went along very well and after 2 hours, they arrived at the town where the orphanage was located. They were allowed to come inside the building and were shown to the office of the director of the orphanage. She was a pleasant and well-spoken lady. After all the introductions were made and they had asked for Niyha, the good news was that he was still living in the orphanage. The lady asked what the reason was for their inquiry about him.

Bart told her in his native language what he had promised to Nihya and that he would like to take him to Canada and that he would like to take care of him. The lady was quite surprised and she asked many questions about Bart's past, what he was doing in Canada and why he would like to take care of his friend.

Doris told the lady that she had adopted Bart and that she knew that Bart had good intentions for his friend.

The director, Mrs. Dijesny, was surprised with Bart's optimism and she liked his honesty. She told Bart and Doris that she would show them where Nihya was at this moment, without him seeing them. Maybe they would not recognize him?

They went to a room with a window where they could see some young men doing artwork at a table. To the surprise of Mrs, Dijesny, Bart told her who Nihya was and that he was happy to see how well his friend was looking. He was almost taller than Bart! When they were back in Mrs. Dijesny's office, she asked Bart and Doris for more information. She promised to talk with Nihya and the authorities about what would and could happen further. It was important that all was done for the benefit of Nihya. Maybe he would not know Bart after all these years? Bart and Doris went to the place where they would stay for the time they were in town, hoping to hear from Mrs. Dijesny with good news. Doris told Bart not to be too optimistic. After all, he had kept his promise.

Chapter 16

The Reunion

After a visit to the farm to see Mushwa, where they had a lunch and a good time looking back on the memories from when Bart was still a young boy and his love for the horses, they came home in the afternoon. Before they could settle down, the telephone rang and it was Mrs. Dijesny. She had some good news and she told them that Nihya would like to see them the next day. Furthermore, he and only he could make the decision about what would happen in his future and with the local authority's approval. They were very happy and told Mrs. Dijesny that they would be there the next day.

When Bart and Doris arrived the next day to meet Nihya, there was so much tension about would happen if he did not recognize Bart. Mrs. Dijesny received them in her office and when they were at ease, she called for Nihya to come in the office.

When he came in to look for Mrs. Dijesny, his eyes fell on Bart and to the amazement of the ladies, he went to Bart and gave him a big hug with tears in his eyes. The friends were reunited and they held each other for a while with tears in their eyes.

Bart asked Nihya if he would like to go with him to Canada and to stay with him. And Nihya said yes and still with more tears in his eyes he said, "You never forgot me and you kept your promise."

Mrs. Dijesny promised to work hard to get permission for Doris and Bart to take Nihya with them to Canada. In the meantime, Bart could visit Nihya in the orphanage he also was told that Nihya's last name was Djin.

Chapter 17

Home to Canada

Papers had to be signed, then a few more formalities with the promise to stay in touch with Mrs. Dijesny. All was taken care of so they were going to book a flight back home.

As it was for Bart a few years before, Nihya could not believe his eyes when they were at the airport. Everything was so overwhelming for him. He was so tense and scared that he had to be calmed down. It was good that he could sleep on the plane. Doris was worried about what would happen if were to change his mind about going but Bart talked with his friend and told him not to worry. He had promised him to take care of him like he did when they were in the orphanage together years ago. Bart said something that Nihja remembered from back then, and it made his friend calm down. Doris was amazed with the patience and devotion of her adopted son.

When Bart had finished his study for accounting and management, he found a good job. He started working for a large company as an assistant in management. He had lots of respect from his superiors not only because of his attitude towards his work but also his nature to the approach of certain problems. One of the company's clients was very happy with his service given and the reorganisation that saved the client lots of money. After a year, Bart was known at the company as 'The Miracle Boy'. And after another year, he was promoted to a higher function in the company that gave him also more responsibility. He, however, was able to carry this. Doris was proud of her son and she prayed every day for the blessings she had received from the Lord.

Chapter 18

Bart and Nihya were living in an apartment in the city of St. Catharines. Nihya had lots of problems getting used to his new environment and Bart worked hard to help him. Doris visited his friend to make sure that he was not lonely. Luckily, he had no major health issues. When Bart was at work, Nihya would stay at home. The biggest problem for Nihya was his language. Bart had a friend who owned a couple of restaurants in town and when he told him about Nihya, his friend told him that he could train and use Nihya as a dishwasher. As a dishwasher, you do not have to speak too much with people. Bart had to drop him off at the restaurant and someone would take him home.

Now, it was up to Bart to help his friend to understand about the work he had to do. Surprisingly, Nihya was eager to get out of the house and he wanted to take the job as a dishwasher in the restaurant. It took a couple of days for him to get acquainted with his new environment but he seemed to love his work, much to Bart's amazement. Every night at home, Nihya would talk about the cooks and the waitresses who were so friendly towards him and how he was happy with the work he had to do. Slowly, Nihya was speaking a little broken English but they all understood what he meant.

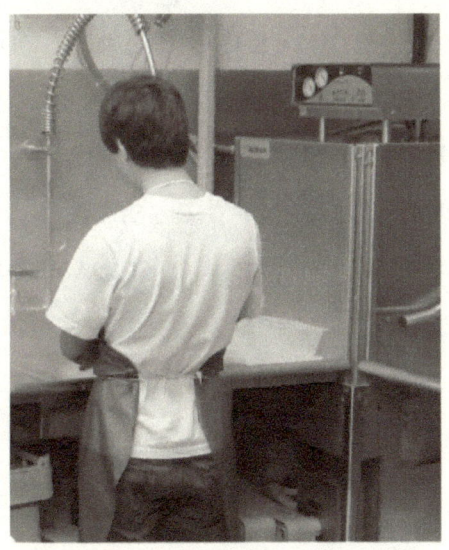

Photo courtesy of Public domain

Nihya as dishwasher

Chapter 19

Bart took his friend Nihya to church every Sunday. In the beginning, it was strange for him but slowly, he was getting used to the people and the ceremonies and preaching in the English language. First, he just sat there and pretended that he knew what was going on. After a few months, Bart noticed that his friend was looking forward going to church and after the service when they were going out for coffee, he knew what was the reason. There was a young woman that Nihya really liked and the feelings were mutual. Her name was Lucy, and she was a few years younger than his friend, good looking but very shy.

On one Sunday, Bart decided to ask Lucy to come for a visit after the service. She liked this idea very much and Nihya was happy and looked forward to meeting her. His English was still not good but he could communicate. Doris was also invited. Bart had bought some delicious pastry and it did not take long before the ice was broken, so to say, and Nihya and Lucy were getting acquainted with each other. Doris was talking to Lucy and Nihya could not keep his eyes off Lucy and when she talked to him, he started to get red in his face. Bart suggested to go out for dinner and they all agreed. Lucy told Bart that she would tell her mother that she would come home a little later and that she was with Doris and family. Doris knew the parents of Lucy so everything was settled. They went to the restaurant where Nihya worked. The evening went very well for Nihya; he started talking to Lucy and he asked her if she wanted to come back next week. She said "Yes Nihya, I would like that very much."

All was going well for Bart.

From the beginning of his work life, Bart started to save his money and had invested some of it in a small business. He had followed this little company from the start and he liked the products they were making and selling. The owner was a friend and both men had been looking for an expansion in the future.

His work, however, took most of his time and the work load was getting larger. On one day, Bart had a great success with one company that needed a big overhaul and he worked hard to save the company from going under. He had great success not only on the financial side but also on the human resources side. The company was going to work more economically and the workers were made partners in the company, which was a miracle. Later, Bart received a big bonus and he invested some of his fortune in a pension fund for his friend Nihya. One more year and Nihya would be able to receive his social benefits. He had his social insurance number and his permanent resident card. So, everything had gone very well for Bart and Doris.

Nihya and Lucy were seeing each other every Sunday and when at the church, they would sit beside each other. Lucy had introduced him to her parents and they were very happy for her. One day, when there was a baptising of some church members, Nihya told Bart that he would like to be baptised someday. He had learned so much about his faith from Lucy. She taught him to read and write English. It took a long time for Nihya but he did his very best. The time went so fast and soon, it was time for Nihya to become a Canadian citizen. Doris looked back at the time they went to get Nihya from the orphanage. Bart and his friend

grew up to be such a good looking and tall men.
She realized she had two sons and she did not
mind. She had also gained a future daughter in law,
Lucy. She felt so blessed with all the things she had
done in her life.

Chapter 20

Bart told Nihya that when he was ready to be baptised, that he would ask to be baptised, also. His friend was so happy and they both decided that it was time to commit themselves to serve the Lord. All their friends and church family were so happy for them. This was something special for the two good friends who grew up in an orphanage and had never forgotten each other and then were reunited in a miraculous way.

A month later, both men were baptised in their church. The Minister had a special service in relation to their experience and that they were an example of what the Lord had promised. Bart had sent a letter to Mushwa wherein he told her all about his decision to serve the Lord and that he was thankful for her educating him when he was a young child.

Chapter 21

Sometimes, Things Don't Go as Expected

There was an economic slow down and the company where Bart was working was affected by this, too. The owners were going to retire so they had sold their business. The new owners were restructuring the company and they had brought in their own people. In their new plans, there was no place for Bart and many people were surprised by this.

It was a disappointment but not something Bart was worried about. He knew that when one door closes, another door will open. He was blessed all these times and he knew that the Lord would take care of him. He had a good record of his work and lots of recommendations from his old clients. He was revaluating himself and did not know what to do in the future.

Bart was out of work for two months and he had no replies to his work applications. Luckily, he was not married and didn't have a family to support. He had spent time with his mother and that was a good thing for her. Doris had missed her adopted son so much and very soon she would retire from her work. She was looking forward to have some grandchildren. Bart had no girlfriend yet and Doris was thinking of all the nice girls in the church.

One day, there was a social event in the church and she invited Bart to go with her. It was not something he was looking forward to but it was going in a wonderful way. At the event, he met a friendly, well spoken girl that he had never met in the church and she kept his attention. When Doris came to see them and was introduced by Bart, everything fell in place, so to say. Betsie was a daughter of one of the church's longest members, a retired CEO of a large international trading company. When they were leaving the party, Doris invited Betsie to come for dinner some day. She gladly accepted the invitation.

Bart was eager to find a good job in his field. He never thought of the company where he had invested his money. One day when he was at home, he had a phone call from his friend Carl, the owner of that company. Bart was so pleased to hear from his friend, Carl, and Carl then offered Bart a job. Bart had to think a moment but told him that he would meet Carl the next day whenever it was convenient for his friend. Everything was going like a dream!

That night Bart fell on his knees and prayed, thanking the Lord for the blessings and that the Lord never had forgotten him. Also, that he was thankful for the opportunity to possibly have work again. He was also thinking of Betsie, something he could not understand. He was looking forward to see her again.

Chapter 22

Bart was looking forward to his meeting with his friend Carl, whom he had not seen for over a year. The meeting went very well. Bart had a pleasant surprise and was offered a job he could not refuse. Carl told him that the company was expanding and that he needed a financial expert like Bart. Bart was to start the next month and he had to get himself acquainted with his new work first to see if he would like the opportunity. There were some very good people he had to work with and that made his new environment so pleasant, something he had not experienced before. The job, however, was new to him and he had to educate himself. There was lots of responsibility and he had to travel a lot. At night, he prayed and asked the Lord for His guidance. Carl's idea was to expand his business to other countries but to get his products exported was not that easy. Bart had to find the right way and to make it economical for Carl's company. One wrong decision would be a disaster. Bart had to do a lot of researching and told Carl that he would like to go Mexico or Europe to find the right company to work with.

It took Bart a month to find the right company that would possibly be a good fit to work with but they had to take a risk. They would have to take a financial part in that company. Bart told his friend that he would like to invest his money in the new venture. Carl agreed and both men made the decision to buy part of an overseas company. Both men were going to travel to meet their new business partners. Bart went home and told Nihya that he was going out of town for a while. At night, he had a lot of praying to do for guidance.

The next day, Doris phoned Bart to tell him that she had invited Betsie for dinner and that she extended the invitation to him as well. He was happy to accept. When he arrived, Betsie was already there and when they were waiting to go to the table, they had a good conversation. Bart felt a warm feeling for her, something strange for him. At dinner, they had a good time and Doris was happy. She knew both young people were interested in each other. Bart told both women about his new job and that he was going out of town for a couple of days. Later, Bart asked if he could bring Betsie to her car which she gladly accepted. They decided to see each other again on Saturday evening. A beautiful relationship had started that would bring lots of happiness in the future.

When Bart went to pick up Betsie to go out for dinner, he met her parents and who were happy to meet him. Doris and Betsie had already talked to them about Bart but when they had seen him, they were satisfied with the choice of her daughter. The dinner went very well and for the first time Bart felt he was in love. After they parted ways for the evening, he was looking forward to see her again.

The next Saturday, he phoned Lucy and asked her how she was doing and told the good news that he had met Betsie. He asked if she and Nihya would like to go out for dinner together. Lucy was happy to accept the invitation.

At dinner, there was more good news from Lucy. She told them that she and Nihya were engaged and had plans for a wedding soon! It was such a big surprise for all of them. But this was not the only good news. Bart looked at Betsie and he took a ring out his pocket and asked her if she would like to marry him. Her answer was "Yes,

Bart, I love you." All their dreams were coming true.

Doris was so happy when she heard the news from all of them. She was blessed with so much happiness. She was thinking back to the time she found her adopted son and how much he had grown to become a wonderful and honest person who always kept his promise. He was just a miracle in her life and others.

Chapter 23

Time was flying by so fast and so much happened in a short time. Nihya and Lucy were going to get married. Bart was his best man and Betsie was one of the bride's maids. The wedding day was planned for a summer day and everything looked so beautiful. Many friends from the church were invited and all went as planned. After dinner, Nihya and Lucy left to go on a honeymoon not too far from their hometown, a gift from Bart. Later, Doris asked Bart when he and Betsie were going to get married. He answered, "Soon, mama."

The business venture of Bart and Carl went very well. The overseas company was growing so fast and they needed an expansion very soon. The company at home could not keep up with all the orders! It became a financially great success and for Carl, a miracle with what Bart had managed to accomplish in such a short time, even in a time of economic slowdown. People working for Carl called him the 'Miracle Boy', not only for what he had done but also for the stability he made in the future of the company. The workers were given a choice to become partners. They also were getting a raise in salary and at the end of the year, a bonus!

Carl and Bart's business was growing in to a world-scale well-known consortium. A year later, Bart became the CEO which was a big honour and also a great responsibility. Bart had become a successful business man and he could look back at so many blessings in his life. He, however, spent most of his fortune helping other people. He donated money to the church to build an addition for a youth auditorium and he started a small scholarship as well.

Chapter 24

Pretty soon, Bart and Betsie were going to get married. The date was set and preparations put in motion. Lucy, Betsie and Doris were working hard in making all the table decorations and other things. The hall was already booked for the wedding. There were many invitations for dinner. Doris, Betsie's parents and all the people working for Carl's company were invited and lots of their church family. A special invitation was sent to Mushwa. Her travel was booked and arrangements made for her to be picked up at the airport. There was also an invitation send to Mrs. Dijesny, but she had to decline.

Bart and Nihya went to the airport and they had made a 'Welcome Mushwa' sign to make it easy for her to recognize them at the arrival terminal. It was very busy at the airport and they had to wait a long time. Most people were already gone and Bart was getting worried. He had given Mushwa his cell phone number and told her that if there was a problem to phone him. Just when they were going to go find out what was wrong, Bart's phone rang and it was a customs agent asking him if he was expecting Mushwa. Bart almost screamed "Yes" and he told them that she had an invitation to his wedding and asked what the problem was. He had to try to be calm otherwise they might make things difficult for them. There was no further delay and Muhswa came through the gate. She had no problem recognizing them. She had a big hug from Bart and the first thing they did was to go for a cup of coffee and to relax before going on the road home. Mushwa could not keep her eyes off the two men, how they have become such wonderful friends. It all was a miracle. On their way home, she had so many questions about what she was seeing.

When they arrived at Bart's home, Doris, Betsie and Lucy were happy to see them. They had so many questions for Mushwa but only Doris and the two men could speak her language. To their surprise, she could speak a little English she had learned from the letters Bart had written to her. Mushwa would stay at the home of Doris for her vacation. Many trips were made to the stores to buy some things she would like to take back home later.

Everything had to be perfect in Doris' eyes because it was her son that was going to be married and, of course, Mushwa understandably felt the same way. Both women were getting along with each other very well. They organized the wedding shower and made lots of delicious food and pastries.

The rehearsal of the wedding went great and everybody involved was up to their task. Nihya was in the wedding party and Carl was Bart's best man. He would have chosen Nihya but his friend was not up to do the job and Bart understood his decision.

The wedding in the church was so beautiful and there were so many people. It was overwhelming for Bart and Betsie, especially the long reception was tiresome. There was lots of fun during the night with speeches from Carl and friends and some mention of the man they called 'The Miracle Boy'.

After dinner, Bart and Betsie were off to St. Kitts in the Caribbean for a two-week long honeymoon.

A limousine brought them to the airport for a much-deserved vacation.

Chapter 25

Coming home from their vacation, Bart and Betsie were invited by Doris for dinner to tell her all about their trip. Nihya and Lucy were invited too. When they had shown everyone their pictures and had told them about their vacation, they were surprised with some great news. Lucy could hardly keep the secret any longer and told them that she was expecting a baby. They were all so happy for Lucy and Nihya. Doris told Betsie that she was going to set a date for a baby shower soon.

When Bart and Betsie went to their home, they were talking about the good news of the evening. Bart was thinking of the joy of having children and was looking forward to have some of his own.

The Next Day, It was Time to Say Goodbye to Mushwa

They were all going to the airport to help her with all the formalities. Bart had made a list of all the things Mushwa was taking home. She would not have any difficulty going through customs, they hoped. A lady going on the same plane to her country promised to take care of Mushwa. It was an emotional goodbye and lots of tears were shed, but they promised to see each other again

Two days later, Bart had a phone call from his former foster parents that everything went well and that Mushwa was home safe.

Chapter 26

Lucy and Nihya's child was born on a warm summer's day, a healthy and beautiful son that they named Christian Mathew Djin. They were so enjoying this little bundle of blessing from the Lord.

Bart realized that he became an uncle and he was excited for his friend and his wife. Nihya was not completely sure what to do but he was learning fast how to put clean diapers on the baby. A few years later, they received the blessing of two more children, identical twin girls.

More Good News, More Blessings

When Bart came home from work, he heard Betsie singing and he was wondering if she was practicing for the choir. When he came into the kitchen, she gave him a big hug and kiss and said "Guess what Bart? I have a surprise!" He did not know what to say and he had no idea what the surprise would be. Then she told him that she was expecting a baby. Bart jumped up and down with joy and gave her another big hug and kiss. He was so happy and later when they were at the table for dinner, they thanked the Lord for all their blessings and for the gift that was coming.

Lots of things had to be done. First the baby's room had to be decorated and made ready. It would be a while before they would know the gender of the baby but everything was set in motion. Betsie had already told Doris and Lucy about the good news but they had to keep it secret until she had told Bart. In the meantime, they were thinking about the names for a boy or for a girl.

Doris was so happy with all that had happened in such a short time. She was going to retire from her work soon and that would be just perfect so she could do babysitting when necessary or just visiting and enjoying her grand children. She could never have dreamed of such things in the past. Now she had two sons, two daughters and in the future, two grand children. What great blessings!

Bart bought one of the restaurants where Niyha was working, from his friend who wanted to slow down and could not handle the work anymore. He had bought it as an investment and he had put it in Nihya's name. He had told Lucy not to tell Nihya and asked her to help him in the financial side of the restaurant. Lucy was working for an accounting firm and it would be easy for her to keep the books. Bart had no idea what was involved in running a business like that. Nihya would have a job and be a future owner. Everything would stay the same and the waitresses still would have their jobs.

Chapter 27

When Bart was at work, he had a phone call from Betsie and she told him to come home because she had to go to the hospital to deliver their baby. Both knew already, from the ultrasound picture, that it would be a girl. Bart was so excited and nervous that he forgot where he had put his car. Betsie told him not to hurry, but he almost drove through a red light. He had to calm himself down so when he brought her to the car, she would not notice how nervous he was. When they drove to the hospital, Betsie kept his mind off the situation and told him that she was talking to Doris who was already there. Later, everything went very well. Bart was a good coach, and they were blessed with a healthy and beautiful baby girl. They gave her the name of Doris and her middle name was Alicia, after Betsie's mother.

A New Chapter in Bart's Life

In the coming month, they were going to be celebrating the anniversary of the friendship of Nihya and Bart. They had known each other for 30 years. They had been reunited after 8 years of being separated. Doris, Lucy and Betsie were organizing a small dinner party in the church for a few close friends. They had invited Mushwa and the teacher from Bart's grade school. It was remarkable that she was still working at the same school. Doris had saved her telephone number. She also had tried to contact Mrs. Dijesny but she was not working in the office anymore.

Bart would pay for the flight of both ladies, but Mushwa could not come this time because her husband was not feeling well. Bart was so eager to meet his teacher again after so many years. He had written her a letter when he married Betsie but after that he had forgotten her. Now he had lots to tell her.

The dinner party was great and Bart's teacher enjoyed her stay with Doris as well as all the news of Bart and his friend, Nihya. She would have never thought that she would experience the great happiness of a little boy who kept the promise he made to his young friend. She told Doris that she loved Bart so much when he was in her class and that it was a miracle and a gift from God Almighty that she could be with them and celebrate the reunion of both young men. After her one-week vacation, she would have liked to stay in Canada but when she thought of the children in her class at home, she was happy to go back.

Chapter 28

Many Opportunities at Work

Carl, the owner of the local company, was planning to retire and he asked Bart to attend a meeting to talk about the future, possible promotions and finding the best people who would be running their business. Both men were the major stockholders of the company and any change would affect the value of this. Later, they would have a meeting with the workers who were also shareholders in the firm.

Carl asked Bart if he would stay on as CEO of their business and he agreed with this. Both men were happy with the solution. They needed to recruit for the positions of manager and an assistant manager. The people working in the office already would have priority if they were qualified.

That same day in the office, Bart had a pleasant surprise. He was nominated and chosen as the Businessman and Humanitarian of the year. It was a great honour and people were calling him, 'The Miracle Boy'.

Bart and Betsie eventually enjoyed the blessing of two children, a girl and a boy named Bart Jr. Lucy and Nihya were blessed with three children, one boy and two girls.

After five more years, Bart wanted to retire from work and spend his time enjoying his life with Betsie and their children. This coming school vacation, they all were going on a cruise with Lucy, Nihya, all their children and with Grandma Doris as well. They were all looking forward to this real family vacation, but it all would be possible if they could find the right people who could take over the work and supervision in both the restaurant and Bart's responsibility of his company. Luckily, everything worked out very well so when the time came, they enjoyed a great vacation and made lots of good memories.

Chapter 29

Finally, Bart was about to retire which meant another person had to be chosen as head of the company. Bart and Carl decided to choose the son of Carl, who was already familiar with running their business and was a devoted, honest and hard worker. He had worked with Bart for the last five years. Still, it would be a great responsibility for this young man but they had great trust in him and also, the people working for him liked him very much.

A dinner party was given in honour of Bart's retirement with all the company workers in attendance. It was a memorable party and some of the workers had great stories to tell. Bart did not know that they had appreciated him so much. He was so thankful for that had happened that he had difficulty to still his emotions.

When Bart came home that night, he felt like he had accomplished a lot in his life and felt so lucky with his wife Betsie and their children and especially with his mom Doris, as she had put all this in motion. He felt so blessed with his friend Nihya, who was so happy. All had gone like a great miracle. He thought back to the time they were in the orphanage and the time that he and Doris went to get his friend as he had promised as a young child. He felt like a Miracle Boy. The Lord had blessed him so much with everything. He was blessed with his mom and his friend Nihya, their families and with his good health. It had been a remarkable journey for both men. It all went in a miraculous way, just the way the Lord had provided.

Epilogue

Doris was enjoying her role of grandma and the grandchildren loved her so much; she always had the time to look after them and play games. Later, when they were in school, she helped them with their studies.

Bart and Nihya were enjoying their retirement. They both loved to go sailing and fishing on the lake and to take vacations with their spouses and children. The restaurant was sold because it became too much for Nihya; he was tired of being a dishwasher. He could enjoy his pension that had built up over the years he was working, thanks to Bart. He was very thankful to know that his friend had done so much for him. They were best friends for life, more like brothers. The Lord had blessed them abundantly. One thing that did not continue in the family and that was the foreign language that was spoken by Doris, Bart and Nihya in the past.

God confirms the steps of the man, whose way He is satisfied with.

<u>A Slogan from the Author</u>

"The way of a good person is like a road map; he will make the wrong turns in life but he will finally reach his destination."